A JIGSAW JONES MYSTERY

The Case of the
Bicycle Bandit

Read more Jigsaw Jones Mysteries by James Preller

A JIGSAW JONES MYSTERY

The Case of the Bicycle Bandit

by James Preller

illustrated by Jamie Smith
cover illustration by R. W. Alley

FEIWEL AND FRIENDS

New York

A Feiwel and Friends Book
An imprint of Macmillan Publishing Group, LLC
175 Fifth Avenue, New York, NY 10010

Our books may be purchased in bulk for promotional, educational, or business
use. Please contact your local bookseller or the Macmillan Corporate and
Premium Sales Department at (800) 221-7945 ext. 5442 or by e-mail at
MacmillanSpecialMarkets@macmillan.com.

Library of Congress Cataloging-in-Publication Data is available.

ISBN 978-1-250-11084-8 (paperback) / ISBN 978-1-250-11083-1 (ebook)

Illustrations by Jamie Smith

Book design by Véronique Lefèvre Sweet

Feiwel and Friends logo designed by Filomena Tuosto

First Feiwel and Friends Edition—2017

Originally published by Scholastic in 2001

Art used with permission from Scholastic

1 3 5 7 9 10 8 6 4 2

mackids.com

For three peas in a pod:
Julian, Sebastian, and Nicholas

CONTENTS

Chapter 1

Old Rusty

"Wait up, Jigsaw!" Ralphie Jordan cried out. "My bike chain slipped off!"

Oh, brother. Not again.

The town library was five minutes from my house. Four minutes if the wind was right. But today it was taking forever—all because of Ralphie Jordan's bicycle.

Ralphie called it "Old Rusty."

I would have called it "Old Hunk of Junk."

Old Rusty could shake and rattle. But it couldn't roll. Not very well, anyway. Its tires were bent. Spokes were missing. The handlebars were twisted. The seat was ripped. The fenders rattled. The brakes squeaked. And worst of all, the chain kept falling off the what-cha-ma-call-it. After every block, Ralphie had to stop. He got off, turned the bicycle upside down, and carefully slipped the chain back onto the round thingy.

I turned and rode back to Ralphie. He was a mess. Grease from the chain covered his face, shirt, and hands. "Maybe we should go home," I offered.

"Hang on," Ralphie said. "Old Rusty will get me there." Ralphie patted Old Rusty on the, er, *rust*, and away we zoomed. At least, I zoomed. Old Rusty sort of crawled. Banging and clanging all the way.

Our teacher, Ms. Gleason, had given us book reports for homework. We had to find a book in the library, read it, and write about it. The book had to be *at least* eighty pages long.

Ralphie chained our bikes to the bike rack and we headed inside. I wandered into the mystery section. Ralphie seemed to wander all over. First, Ralphie stared into the fish tank, making goofy faces and *glub-glub* sounds. Then he walked along, picked up a book, turned to the last page, frowned, and put it back. Over and over again.

"What are you doing, Ralphie?" I asked.

"Just looking," he said.

"What kind of book are you looking for?"

"A short one," Ralphie replied. "And I just found it." He held up a book. It was called *Plastic: Yesterday, Today, and Tomorrow.*

"You want to do a report on . . . plastic?" I asked.

Ralphie opened the book to the last page. "Look, exactly eighty pages—and it has lots of pictures, too."

I sighed and kept searching in the mystery section. After all, I was a detective.

For a dollar a day, I made problems go away. I loved everything about mysteries—the clues, the secret codes, the disguises, everything. I even loved mystery stories. I picked out an Encyclopedia Brown.

We checked out our books and went outside.

At the bike rack, Ralphie stopped suddenly. "My bike!" he exclaimed. "It's g-g-gone!"

The Scene of the Crime

Ralphie's lower lip trembled. He blinked back tears. "Where's Old Rusty?" he asked me.

But Ralphie already knew the answer. He just couldn't believe it. Somebody had stolen Ralphie's bike.

I was lucky. My bike was still there.

I pulled my detective journal from my backpack. I wrote:

THE CASE OF THE BICYCLE BANDIT

"Wait here," I told Ralphie. "Don't touch anything. I'm going inside to call Mila. We'll need her help."

I told Mila to get down to the library, fast.

"How fast?" she asked.

"Like, yesterday," I replied.

"I'll be right there," Mila answered.

I went back outside. Ralphie was sitting on the ground, cross-legged. His chin was buried in his hands.

While we waited for Mila, I drew a quick sketch. When you're a detective, it's important to study the scene of the crime.

That's how you find clues. There were five bicycles in the rack. Mine was brand-new, not a hand-me-down like Ralphie's. I used to ride my brother Nicholas's beat-up old bike. Then I helped pay for a new one with the money I earned from my detective business. It was a Cobra Daredevil with a banana-yellow frame.

"That's weird," I said. "Isn't this your lock, Ralphie?"

Ralphie nodded. "Yeah."

"I thought you locked up *both* bikes."

"I did," Ralphie answered.

I didn't argue. But facts were facts. Here was my bike, locked up with Ralphie's chain. His bike was gone. Maybe Ralphie had locked up only my bike by mistake.

Mila pulled up, slamming on the brakes. Her back wheel skidded on the cement. Ralphie barely noticed. He stared at the empty space in the bike rack, frowning.

Mila is my partner. Together, we solve mysteries. We've found missing hamsters, stolen baseball cards, lost sleds. We've even tangled with phony lake monsters and runaway dogs. But a stolen bicycle—that was something new. "All right," she said. "Tell me what happened."

I told Mila what we knew. She listened carefully, arms folded across her chest. "The bandit was lucky," I said. "It looks like Ralphie forgot to lock his bicycle."

Mila nodded. "*Looks* that way."

Ralphie protested. "Don't blame me. I locked up *both* bikes. I know I did. *I know it.*"

Mila bit her lip. She put her hand on Ralphie's shoulder. "No one is blaming you," she soothed. "You're right to feel mad. Stealing a bicycle—that's like the worst thing on earth. Only a real creep would do something like that."

Ralphie sniffed and looked away. His eyes followed a bird circling in the sky. It

circled once, twice, three times. Then it flew off.

Leaving behind an empty sky.

"A real creep," Ralphie muttered in agreement.

Chapter 3

Witnesses

"What time is it?" I asked.

Ralphie glanced at his bare wrist. "Half past my freckle," he gloomily replied.

I couldn't help but smile. And Ralphie couldn't help but say funny things. With him, it was like breathing. Ralphie even made jokes when nobody felt like laughing.

"Let's see if there were any witnesses," Mila suggested. She gestured toward the grassy lawn beyond the bike racks. There was a lady walking a small dog with shaggy white fur. That is, the *dog* had shaggy white fur. The lady's hair was shaggy and black. There was a freckle-faced teenager with red hair leaning against a tree. I caught him looking in our direction. He quickly turned away to watch some girls playing Frisbee. Behind us, a man on a bench sat reading a newspaper. A round hat sat beside him, like an old friend.

I turned to Ralphie. "You better leave the detective work to us," I said. "Do you want to borrow my bike to get home?"

Ralphie shook his head. "No, I'll walk. Might as well get used to it." Ralphie's eyes suddenly widened. "Hey, there's David Chang. He's on my brother Justin's basketball team. Maybe I can walk home with him."

Ralphie ran up to David, who was leaving the library. I watched Ralphie gesture and point to the bike rack. He was telling David the whole sad story. I walked over. Ralphie introduced us. "Jigsaw is a detective," Ralphie bragged. "He'll get my bike back."

David looked about fourteen years old. He had a helmet in one hand and a skateboard under the other arm. David shifted uncomfortably under the weight of his backpack. I asked him if he had noticed anyone strange inside the library. "Nah, I just dropped off a few books and scrammed," he answered. "It's too nice to hang inside."

I watched them walk away. Actually, only Ralphie walked. David cruised alongside

him on his skateboard. He stopped, handed Ralphie his backpack, and got back on the skateboard. What a guy, I thought. David made Ralphie carry his heavy backpack!

Across the field, Mila was standing with the lady and her dog. Mila bent down and tried to pet the dog. But it was one of those tiny, nervous dogs. It yapped at Mila and snapped its sharp little teeth. Mila pulled her hand away and growled back.

The man on the bench was nice enough. He said he'd been reading and hadn't seen anything. He laughed. "Once I start reading, we could have an earthquake and I wouldn't notice."

I thanked him anyway. I wrote his name in my journal, just in case: MAX KORNSTEIN. When I turned around, Mila was talking to the Frisbee players. They seemed to be shaking their heads. The red-haired boy stood up to leave on his skateboard. "Wait up!" I called. "I need to talk to you!"

The boy glanced over his shoulder. He put a hand to his ear and shook his head. Like he couldn't hear me. Then he pushed off hard with his right foot. *Zoom.*

He left me in the dust.

Go figure.

Chapter 4

Suspect on Wheels

I awoke Sunday morning to find a note on my doorstep.

tree	house	the	case	message
the	at	of	destroy	secret
in	noon	facts	this	the
meet	to	the	note	solve
let's	go	over	after	you

I started reading it: *tree house the case message the at of . . .*

It didn't make any sense. That could only

mean one thing. It was a message from Mila. She always wrote her notes in code.

I searched my brain for all the codes I knew. Believe me, it was crowded in there. Secret codes are a part of the business. You can't be a detective without them. I knew mirror codes and color codes, space codes and list codes. Suddenly it hit me. This was an up-and-down code. Instead of reading from left to right, you had to start at the bottom of the first column, read up, then go over to the next column and read down, then over, then up again.

I figured out the message. Then it was time to destroy the note. That's where my trusty dog, Rags, came in. He'd eat anything. I spread peanut butter on it. Rags was happy to help.

There was a full glass of grape juice waiting for Mila later that morning when she climbed the tree house ladder. She was singing "Let's Go Fly a Kite" from *Mary*

Poppins. As usual, she changed the words around:

> *"Let's go ride a bike*
> *Up to the highest height!*
> *Let's go ride a bike*
> *And send it . . ."*

Mila stopped singing and scratched her nose. "Hey, Jigsaw. What rhymes with *soaring?*"

"Pouring?" I offered. "Snoring?"

Mila sang again:

> *"Let's go ride a bike*
> *It sure . . . beats . . . snoring!"*

"You're nuts," I observed.

Mila shrugged. "Maybe."

"Let's get down to business," I said. "Any luck with the witnesses?"

"Not really," Mila said. "And I almost got bit, too," she added.

I smiled. "Yeah, that little dog seemed angry."

"Actually, the lady said the dog, Mr. Pickles, was scared."

"Scared of *you*?" I laughed.

"Not me," Mila said. "Mr. Pickles almost got run over by a skateboarder."

"Oh?"

"Yeah. The lady was upset about it. She said three kids came racing down the sidewalk and almost flattened Mr. Pickles."

"Three kids?" I asked. "On skateboards?"

Mila opened her little memo pad. She read out loud: "'Three teenagers on skateboards . . .'"

"I saw two kids with skateboards at the library," I recalled. "I wonder if it was them? And if it was, *who* was the third kid? And *where* was he?"

We let that question wander past like a lonely cloud. I suddenly remembered David Chang. His backpack was large and bulky. I told Mila about it.

"It must have been filled with books," Mila concluded.

"Nope," I said. "He told me he dropped off a few books and scrammed."

Mila twisted the ends of her long black hair. "Are you sure his backpack was full?"

"I think so," I said. "He made Ralphie carry it. We can check with him."

I wrote in my journal:

What was in David Chang's backpack?

Mila looked over my shoulder as I wrote. "David couldn't have stolen the bike. You saw him leave the library."

"Yes," I said. "But the lady saw *three* kids ride skateboards to the library. Only two left on skateboards. What happened to the other kid?"

Mila stared at me, blinking. "Do you think . . . ?"

I nodded. It was exactly what I thought. "Maybe he's the one who took Ralphie's bicycle."

"But what about his skateboard?" Mila asked. "You can't ride a bike and carry a skateboard at the same time."

I gulped down the last of my grape juice. "I think David Chang may know the answer."

Chapter 5

Justin

We found Ralphie Jordan in his driveway. He was shooting hoops with his older brother, Justin.

Just as Ralphie went to shoot, Justin soared high into the air. *WHAP!* He blocked the shot and sent the ball flying into the bushes. Then Justin sank three long bombs—*swish, swish, swish*—and the game was over.

"I'm gonna beat you one day," Ralphie promised. "Just you wait."

Justin just laughed and gave Ralphie a

playful shove. Of course, we attacked. Ralphie pounced on Justin's legs. Mila jumped on his back, driving Justin to the ground. I twisted his fingers into pretzels.

"Need a hand?" a voice asked.

We stopped. It was David Chang.

"I've got it under control," Justin replied. *Wham, bam*. He stacked us up like pancakes and pinned us to the ground. It felt like he was a steamroller—and we were the road.

Ouch.

Justin stood up, puffing slightly. "You guys are getting tough," he said. "But not tough enough. I'd love to hang around, but I've got things to do."

He got his skateboard out of the garage. "Hey, Ralphie," he called out. "You can borrow my bike if you want."

"Maybe, sure, thanks," Ralphie mumbled.

"Hey, little brother," Justin said. "Don't stress about your bike. I'm sure it will turn up in a few days."

Ralphie frowned. "Old Rusty is gone forever," he sighed.

"No way," Justin said, jerking a thumb toward Mila and me. "You'll get Old Rusty back. You've got top detectives on the case." He gave us a wink.

"Where are you guys going, anyway?" Ralphie asked Justin and David.

"Out," Justin said. He strapped on his helmet.

I spoke up. "Do you guys know a kid with bright red hair? He's about your age, maybe older. He's got a lot of freckles."

David glanced at Justin.

"Lots of kids have freckles," Justin answered.

David wheeled around on his skateboard and raced down the driveway. Justin had fancier moves. He zigged and zagged,

leaning hard to his left then right. His arms were stretched out to his sides. Very cool.

"Your brother's nice," Mila observed.

"Yeah, most of the time," Ralphie agreed. "He likes to kid around a lot."

I laughed. "Remember the phony ghost? Justin had us fooled for a while."

We sat under a tree and laughed about it. A while back Justin pretended he was a ghost. He had Ralphie nearly scared out of his boxer shorts. Fortunately, Mila and I solved the mystery.

Teenagers. Yeesh.

Ralphie wanted to pay us for our work. But there was one problem. He didn't get his allowance until the end of the week.

"This one's a freebie," I said. "But remember us if you win the lottery."

"Do you have any suspects?" Ralphie asked.

"Maybe," I answered. "There's one kid on a skateboard I'd like to track down. Unfortunately, the best witness is a dog named Mr. Pickles."

"Huh?"

"Don't worry about it, Ralphie," I said. "We'll get your bike back. I promise."

"One last thing, Ralphie," Mila said. "About David's backpack. Do you know what was in it?"

Ralphie tilted his head, thinking. "Oh, yeah. It was a skateboard."

"He had *two* skateboards?" I asked.

"Yeah," Ralphie said. "Weird, huh. He said he was holding it for a friend."

Mila and I exchanged looks.

"Weird, huh," she repeated.

I scratched the back of my neck. I had an itch to learn more about David Chang.

Chapter 6

Art Class

All the kids in room 201 were mad about Ralphie's bike.

"It's horrible!"

"It's terrible!"

"It's horribly terrible!"

"It's terribly horrible!"

They all promised to help. Everyone crowded around Ralphie, trying to cheer him up.

"Um, like, maybe your father will, like, buy you a new one," Lucy Hiller said.

"Don't want a new one," Ralphie flatly stated. "I like Old Rusty just fine. It was a hand-me-down from Justin. Besides, my dad says I can't get a new bike until my birthday."

"When's that?" Mila asked.

"July twelfth," groaned Ralphie. "About a million days from now."

"Have you tried begging?" Bobby Solofsky suggested.

Nicole Rodriguez piped up. "Bobby's right. Begging works. I learned that from our dog, Zippy. The trick is to try to look as much like a puppy as possible."

"Been there, done that," scoffed Ralphie. "I'm an expert." He dropped down to his knees, bent his hands before his chest like a hungry pooch, and whined, *"Nnnnn, nnnnn, nnnnn!"*

We all laughed. Ralphie brushed himself off. "Begging doesn't work with my dad. He just throws me a doggy snack."

At recess, I fooled around on the monkey bars with Eddie Becker and Bigs Maloney. "We don't get it," Eddie Becker said, hanging upside down by his knees. "Why would anybody steal Ralphie's bike?"

"It's a piece of junk," Bigs noted.

They were right. Why would anyone want a junker like Old Rusty? There's never a crime without a reason. What was the *motive*? Who would want an old, broken-down bicycle?

"Ralphie says he locked up *both* bikes," I said.

Bigs jumped to the ground. His big feet crashed like thunder. "No way," Bigs said. "The bandit would have taken your bike, Jigsaw. Your Cobra Daredevil is awesome."

I thanked Bigs for the kind words. The bell rang. We lined up to go inside. But a voice in my head kept repeating: *What if Ralphie was right about locking up both*

bikes? It was a piece I couldn't fit into the puzzle.

Ralphie had to be wrong, I concluded. No robber would unlock the bikes, take Ralphie's, then lock mine back up. It made no sense.

We had art with Mr. Manus on Mondays. Today, he encouraged us to draw whatever we wanted. I drew a picture of Rags.

RAGS
Dog Detective

Mr. Manus says we all have unique talents. Some people, like Joey Pignattano, are good at drawing flowers and trees. Kim Lewis is good at cars and trucks. And Geetha Nair, well, she can draw faces. That day, she drew an awesome picture of Bigs Maloney. It looked just like him.

Mr. Manus held it up for everyone to admire. "This goes up on the board," he announced.

That's when Mila came up with a terrific idea. She whispered to Geetha, "Do you really want to help on the case?"

Geetha rarely spoke. She was very shy. Instead, she silently nodded.

Yes.

Chapter 7

Geetha and Mr. Pickles

Yap, yap-yap! Bark-bark, barkbarkbarkbark!!!

I groaned into Mila's ear, "Mr. Pickles, I presume."

The door opened. The witness from the library, Mrs. Flint, smiled at Mila. Mr. Pickles jumped up and down by her feet, yapping loudly.

Bark-bark, grrrrr, barkbarkbarkbark!!!

Geetha stepped behind me.

"Don't worry about Mr. Pickles," Mrs. Flint said cheerfully. "He's just excited."

The little furball jumped up and down.

Mrs. Flint bent down until she was nose to nose with Mr. Pickles. "No, Mr. Pickles! NO!" she screamed.

"We don't mind," I lied. "Mr. Pickles is just, er, lively." I bent down to pet Mr. Pickles. He snapped at my hand like a hungry wolf.

"Down, Mr. Pickles! DOWN!" screamed Mrs. Flint. "I'm so sorry," she fretted, shoving Mr. Pickles away with her foot. "I'll put Mr. Pickles in the basement."

I thought that was a terrific idea.

Mrs. Flint led us to a screened back porch. It was filled with plants and strange flowers. "Welcome to my jungle," Mrs. Flint said, offering us lemonade and cookies.

"This is Geetha Nair," I explained, gesturing to Geetha. "She's an artist."

Geetha smiled politely at her shoes. She rested a large artist's pad on her lap. In her fist she clutched a bundle of colored pencils.

Mila explained the plan. We wanted Mrs.

Flint to describe the skateboarders. While she talked, Geetha would try to draw a picture of them.

"Oh, how thrilling!" Mrs. Flint said, snapping into a cookie. "Just like on television!"

I coughed. "This is for real," I reminded her.

We already knew the identity of the first skateboarder. That was David Chang. Mrs. Flint described him perfectly. I winked at Mila. Mrs. Flint was a good witness.

"What about the others?" I prodded.

Mrs. Flint gobbled down another cookie. A few crumbs fell to her lap. She closed her eyes and spoke: "Bright red hair . . . very curly . . . freckles . . . a little pug nose, like a piglet. . . ."

Geetha asked a few questions. She wanted to know the shape of his head, his eyes, his mouth. I looked at her sketchpad.

"Wow, that's him!" I said, remembering the boy at the library.

"Great," Mila said. "Now we can show the picture around. Somebody is bound to know his name."

"What about the third skateboarder?" I asked.

Mrs. Flint frowned. "He wore a sweatshirt with a hood. I didn't get a good look at him."

The sweatshirt was dark green, she told us. And the boy was taller than the other two. That was all she knew. We gobbled down the last of the cookies and left.

Once outside, I turned to Mila. "We've got to find the third skateboarder."

Mila pointed at Geetha's picture of the red-haired boy. "Let's find *him* first. I think he'll lead us to the boy with the green sweatshirt."

"Great work," I thanked Geetha. "You've been a big help."

Geetha stared hard at the ground.

Slowly, ever so slightly, the corners of her mouth turned up into a smile.

The Hooded Rider

$2 REWARD
Do you know this boy?
Call 555-4523

We made ten copies of Geetha's picture.
Mila printed the words. Danika Starling and

Kim Lewis hung up the posters all over town. Everybody in our class chipped in for the reward—even Ms. Gleason.

I got a phone call the very next day.

It was from a third grader named Shirley Hitchcock. "I know the kid in the poster," she announced.

"Keep talking," I said.

"His name is Snarky Smithers. Everybody calls him the Snarkster."

"What's his address?" I asked.

"Do I get the reward?"

"Yes," I answered. "*After* you give me the address."

Shirley told me where he lived.

"How do you know him?" I asked.

"He lives on my block," Shirley explained.

"What else do you know?"

"He's a grease monkey," Shirley said.

"A grease monkey?"

"Yeah. The Snarkster loves building things. He takes things apart and puts them

together again. Old radios, toasters, bicycles, go-carts . . ."

"Bicycles?" I asked. "What do you mean?"

Shirley told me that Snarky Smithers ran a little business. He bought old, junky bikes at garage sales—cheap. Then he fixed them up and sold them. "He's very talented," Shirley added.

I ate a bowl of Frosted Flakes in the kitchen. They tasted *grrreeat!* While I ate, I wrote in my detective journal. Like a jigsaw puzzle, the case was coming together. The clues were starting to fit into place.

THREE SUSPECTS
1) David Chang
2) Snarky Smithers
3) The Hooded Rider

I put a star next to number two. I asked myself, What do I know about Snarky Smithers?

I wrote down:

- Snarky builds bicycles.
- Motive? Spare parts!
- He could have used Old Rusty!

I began to wonder if it was a three-man job. I thought back to the day of the robbery. David Chang was *inside* the library. Snarky Smithers was *outside* the library. A witness saw David and Snarky together. But someone else took Old Rusty.

Maybe they all worked as a team.

Maybe David and Snarky were the lookouts.

It all depended on the hooded rider. We had to find him—soon.

I called Ralphie Jordan's house.

No one was home.

I had no luck at Mila's, either.

Oh, well. I'd have to go alone.

I went to the basement and spilled out my box of detective supplies. There it was—the Super Spy Scope X-2000. I pulled my cap down tight and left the house.

I was on my way to 211 Coconut Grove.

It was time to spy on Snarky Smithers.

Chapter 9

The Stakeout

There was a tree across the street from 211 Coconut Grove. I pulled the straps on my backpack tight. Then up I climbed. A squirrel chittered angrily from a nearby branch. He didn't like sharing the tree, I supposed.

The X-2000 was the ultimate spying machine. It worked like binoculars. But it also had "special extender action." I could use it to see around corners.

In the detective business, we called this a stakeout. You watch and wait, hidden from

sight. Twenty minutes later the hooded rider rolled up on a skateboard. I couldn't see his face. He rang the doorbell. The door opened and there was the red-haired boy, Snarky Smithers. They walked together around the front of the house, opened the garage door, and went inside.

The door closed before I could get a good look inside. But I saw enough—bicycles, lots of bicycles. I saw that the garage had a side window. I counted to thirty. *One banana, two banana, three banana* . . . Then I jumped from the tree.

I made my way across the street. There were bushes on the side of the garage. I ducked down behind them. Ouch. Prickers. Slowly, silently, I pulled the X-2000 to its longest reach. I pointed the scope at the window.

The Snarkster faced the hooded rider. They were talking. Snarky was frowning, gesturing with his hands. The hooded

rider's back was to me. I wanted to put my ear to the windowpane to listen, but I didn't dare.

I felt something brush against me. I quickly spun around and lost my balance, tapping the X-2000 against the window. *Meow.* A black cat sat nearby, licking its paws. Bad, bad luck. I froze and held my breath.

Thirty bananas later, I peeked inside again. The Snarkster was gone! My eyes

searched from side to side. Did he hear me? Was he coming after me?

A door leading from inside the garage to the house opened. It was Snarky, coming back into the garage. He had something in his hand. The hooded rider held out a hand. One, two, three, four. Snarky counted out four dollar bills. They might have been ones, fives, or tens. I couldn't tell which. But one thing was sure: Snarky was paying him for something.

They shook hands and turned to leave. I made myself small behind the bushes. Crawling across the ground, I slid the scope of the X-2000 beyond the wall. The Snarkster yawned, scratched himself, and went into the house.

The hooded rider skateboarded down the driveway. Arms stretched out to his sides, he zigged and zagged, leaning hard to his left and right.

It hit me like a brick.

I knew the hooded rider.

Chapter 10

Trapped!

I lay still for a few more minutes. Maybe I was waiting for the coast to clear. Maybe I was playing it safe. Or maybe I was just plain scared.

The garage was empty.

But the door was still open.

I knew what I had to do.

I took a deep breath and entered the garage.

It was cluttered with tools and bicycles. There was a pile of old tires. Spray-paint cans. Old bicycle parts strewn on the floor.

It was more like a workshop than a garage. There wasn't room for a car.

I crept up to the door that led into the house. I pressed my ear against it. I heard muffled sounds. The shuffling of feet. A chair scraping on the floor. The clink of a spoon against a dish. The kitchen, I decided. Snarky Smithers was in there, eating a snack.

I turned my gaze to the bicycles. I noticed one that looked familiar. Could it be? It *might* have been Old Rusty. But this bike wasn't rusty anymore. It had a new seat, new handlebars, new pedals. The spokes seemed shiny and clean. The frame was a shiny, sparkling blue. I sniffed it. Fresh paint. Still wet.

I was just about to get out of there when I heard a faint *clomp, clomp*. The sound of footsteps, coming closer, just on the other side of the door. I froze in place—and watched the doorknob slowly, slowly turn.

The Snarkster. He was coming into the garage!

I dove into the darkest corner and ducked down behind a few boxes. I heard the door open. Snarky entered the garage.

"Hmmmm, what's this?" he wondered aloud.

My heart beat faster. *Thumpa-thump, thumpa-thump, thumpa-thump.* I peeked around the box. Snarky was holding

something, turning it over in his hands. It was my Super Spy Scope X-2000! I'd left it on the ground beside Old Rusty. Snarky was suspicious. He looked around the garage. "Hello?" he called out. "Anybody here?"

He took a step toward me.

Then another.

Now my heart was a bass drum. *BOOM, BOOM, BOOM!* I closed my eyes and . . .

. . . *Bbbrrring. Bbbrrring-bbbring!*

The phone!

Answer it, I prayed. Go on, Snarky. Answer the phone!

Snarky paused. He looked toward the kitchen door. *Bbbrrring-bbbring.* He took another step toward me, muttered, then tossed the X-2000 onto a shelf. He went inside to answer the phone.

I didn't stick around to see what happened next. I jumped up—whoops, *CRASH!*—and knocked over a bicycle.

"Who's that?!" Snarky called out from the kitchen.

I grabbed the X-2000.

And never looked back.

I just ran. And ran. And ran.

Chapter 11

Confess!

My first stop was Mila's house.

We sat together on the steps of her front stoop. I told her about my adventures.

"Are you absolutely sure it was Justin?" Mila asked.

"Almost," I said. "All the clues point to him." I ticked them off on my fingers. "First, the way he rode the skateboard. It was just like Justin."

Mila went, "Hmmmm."

"Second, we already know that he's friends with David Chang. Third, I think

Ralphie was right all along. He *did* lock up both bikes. But it didn't matter."

"Explain," Mila said.

"Old Rusty was a hand-me-down," I said. "A hand-me-down bicycle with a hand-me-down lock. Justin knew the combination!"

"I get it," Mila said. "That's why your bike was still there. Justin locked it back up. He only wanted Old Rusty."

I flicked a pebble with my thumb. "Exactly."

"But . . . *why*?" Mila asked.

"Why?" I echoed.

"Why take his own brother's bike? Why not your bike? If he was going to sell it to this Snarkster fellow, wouldn't he get more money for a new bike?"

I frowned. "Please, Mila. Get real. I'm a detective. Nobody wants to steal from a detective.

"Anyway," I said glumly. "It has to be Justin. But we need more proof."

We found Ralphie and Justin at home, watching television. I asked to use the bathroom. I went into the bathroom and flicked on the light. I turned on the water to make it sound like I was washing my hands. Then I snuck across the hall into Justin's room. I found what I was looking for in his closet. A green hooded sweatshirt—with grease stains. The loose bike chain, of course! It was all the proof I needed.

Now I had to confront Justin. I went back and challenged him to a wrestling match. "Nah, too busy," Justin replied, staring at the TV.

"Chicken," I said, flapping my arms like wings. "*Bawk-ba-bawk.*"

That did it. Ten seconds later, we were out on the front lawn. Mila and Ralphie followed us out. Justin put my head into a hammerlock. *Wham!* He flung me to the ground.

I whispered into his ear. *"I know you stole it."*

Justin's eyes narrowed. He tightened the hammerlock.

"Don't say another word," he threatened. "Or you'll ruin everything."

I wasn't exactly having a wonderful time. Hammerlocks have that effect on me.

Justin leaned close to me. "You don't understand," he hissed through gritted teeth. "Trust me."

I did what I had to do.

"Confess!" I screamed. "Tell Ralphie the TRUTH!"

Chapter 12

Big Blue

"Tell me what?" Ralphie asked. "What are you blabbering about, Jigsaw?"

Justin stood up. He glared down at me. I didn't care. I was too busy fumbling around on the ground, making sure my head was still attached to my body.

Justin held up five fingers. "Give me five minutes. First I have to make a phone call."

"What's going on?" Ralphie asked.

"Just wait," I said, rubbing my neck.

A minute later, Justin wheeled down the driveway on his skateboard. "I'll be right back," he shouted. "Jigsaw, don't say another word."

Poor Ralphie looked totally confused. He asked, "What's going on, guys?"

"*Mmmmmmmrrrrrrffff, mmmmmmrrrrrfffff,*" I mumbled.

"He can't talk," Mila observed.

Five minutes came and went. Ten minutes. Fifteen. Finally, Justin rode up on a sparkling blue bicycle. It had a new seat, new handlebars, new pedals. The spokes were shiny and clean.

Even the paint was dry.

Justin climbed off the bike and handed it to Ralphie. "Here," he said. "Call it an early birthday present." Justin glanced at me and smirked. He didn't seem angry.

Ralphie's jaw dropped open. "A new bike? For me?"

"Look closer, little brother. It's Old Rusty— new and improved. I paid someone to fix it up."

My eardrums almost burst from Ralphie's wild, happy screams.

Justin explained everything. "I wanted to surprise you," he told Ralphie. "I thought it would be cool if you thought it was stolen. That would make you even happier when you got Old Rusty back."

Ralphie finally understood. "*You* stole Old Rusty?!" he said, disbelieving.

Justin nodded toward Mila and me. "Ask the detectives," he said. "They have it all figured out."

Ralphie gazed happily at Old Rusty. "It was a rotten trick," he told Justin. "Worse than the phony ghost."

Justin smiled. "Maybe. But you *loved* the ghost trick. Admit it. I make life more interesting for you guys. Besides, aren't you happy now?"

Ralphie smiled wide. "Thanks—thanks a whole lot. You're the best big brother I've got."

"I'm the *only* big brother you've got, pal," Justin said with a laugh.

"Hold on," Mila said to Justin. "Jigsaw saw the Snarkster pay *you*. How do you explain that?"

"Pay me?" Justin asked. He shot me a look.

"I spied on you," I confessed. "In Snarky's garage."

Justin smiled. "You've got guts, Jigsaw. I have to give you credit. But I'm the one who paid Snarky. Maybe you saw him give me eight dollars change." He reached into his pocket and pulled out a five and three one-dollar bills.

Ralphie snatched the money from Justin's hands. He handed it to me.

"Hey!" Justin complained.

"Hay is for horses," Ralphie said. "But this money is for Jigsaw and Mila. They earned it."

Justin's face slowly broke into a smile.

"You're right, Ralphie. I guess maybe it was a nasty trick after all. Do you forgive me?"

"Forgive you?" Ralphie said. "This is one of the happiest days of my life!"

He gave his brother a high five.

The case of the bicycle bandit was solved. Ralphie was smiling again. He had Old Rusty back, which he now called "Big Blue." And it turned out that he had a pretty terrific brother after all.

I whispered something to Mila. She smiled. "Great idea, Jigsaw."

So I waved the eight dollars in the air. "Let's celebrate with ice cream," I said. "It's our treat!"

Don't miss this special sneak peek at
a brand-new, never-before-published
JIGSAW JONES MYSTERY:

The Case from
Outer Space

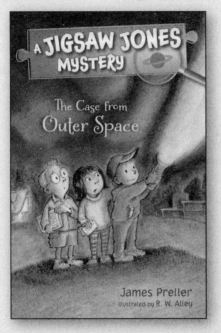

When **Joey** and **Danika** find a mysterious note
tucked inside a book, all signs point to a visitor
from outer space. Yikes! Can Jigsaw solve this
case, when the clues are out of this world?

Chapter 1

A Knock on the Door

Call me Jones.

Jigsaw Jones, private eye.

I solve mysteries. For a dollar a day, I make problems go away. I've found stolen bicycles, lost jewelry, and missing parakeets. I've even tangled with dancing ghosts and haunted scarecrows.

Mysteries can happen anywhere, at any time. One thing I've learned in this business is that anyone is a suspect. That includes friends, family, and a little green man from outer space.

Go figure.

It was a lazy Sunday morning. Outside my window, it looked like a nice spring day. The sky was blue with wispy clouds that looked like they had been painted by an artist. A swell day for a ball game. Or a mystery. Maybe both if I got lucky.

I was standing at my dining room table, staring at a 500-piece jigsaw puzzle. It was supposed to be a picture of our solar system. The sun and eight planets. But right now it was a mess. Scattered pieces lay everywhere. I scratched my head and munched on a blueberry Pop-Tart. Not too hot, not too cold. *Just right.* As a cook, I'm pretty good with a toaster. I began working on the border, grouping all the pieces that had a flat edge. Sooner or later, I'd work my way through the planets. The rust red of Mars. The rings of Saturn. And the green tint of Neptune. I've never met a puzzle I couldn't

solve. That's because I know the secret. The simple trick? Don't give up.

Don't ever give up.

My dog, Rags, leaped at the door. He barked and barked. A minute later, the doorbell rang. *Ding-a-ling, ding-dong.* That's the thing about Rags. He's faster than a doorbell. People have been coming to our house all his life. But for my dog, it's always the most exciting thing that ever happened.

Every single time.

"Get the door, Worm," my brother Billy said. He was sprawled on the couch, reading a book. Teenagers, yeesh.

"Why me?" I complained.

"Because I'm not doing it."

Billy kept reading.

Rags kept barking.

And the doorbell kept ringing.

Somebody was in a hurry.

I opened the door. Joey Pignattano and Danika Starling were standing on my stoop.

We were in the same class together, room 201, with Ms. Gleason.

"Hey, Jigsaw!" Danika waved. She bounced on her toes. The bright beads in her hair clicked and clacked.

"Boy, am I glad to see you!" Joey exclaimed. He burst into the room. "Got any water?"

"I would invite you inside, Joey," I said, "but you beat me to it."

Danika smiled.

"I ate half a bag of Jolly Ranchers this morning," Joey announced. "Now my tongue feels super weird!"

"That's not good for your teeth," I said.

Joey looked worried. "My tongue isn't good for my teeth? Are you sure? They both live inside my mouth."

"Never mind," I said.

"Pipe down, guys!" Billy complained. "I'm reading here."

"Come into the kitchen," I told Joey and Danika. "We'll get fewer complaints. Besides, I've got grape juice. It's on the house."

"On the house?" Joey asked. "Is it safe?"

I blinked. "What?"

"You keep grape juice on your roof?" Joey asked.

Danika gave Joey a friendly shove. "Jigsaw said 'on the house.' He means it's free, Joey," she said, laughing.

Joey pushed back his glasses with an index finger. "Free? In that case, I'll take a big glass."

Chapter 2

One Small Problem

I poured three glasses of grape juice.

"Got any snacks?" Joey asked. "Cookies? Chips? Corn dogs? Crackers?"

"Corn dogs?" I repeated. "Seriously?"

"Oh, they are delicious," Joey said. "I ate six yesterday. Or was that last week? I forget."

Danika shook her head and giggled. Joey always made her laugh.

I set out a bowl of chips.

Joey pounced like a football player on a

fumble. He was a skinny guy, but he ate like a rhinoceros.

"So what's up?" I asked.

"We found a note," Danika began.

"Aliens are coming," Joey interrupted. He chomped on a fistful of potato chips.

I waited for Joey to stop chewing. It took a while. *Hum-dee-dum, dee-dum-dum.* I finally asked, "What do you mean, aliens?"

"Aliens, Jigsaw!" he exclaimed. "Little green men from Mars—from the stars—from outer space!"